Christmas
with the
Mice Next Door

Anthony Knowles

Illustrated by
Susan Edwards

MACMILLAN CHILDREN'S BOOKS

for
Oliver and Samuel
and for my mother

First published in Great Britain 1990 by
MACMILLAN CHILDREN'S BOOKS
A division of Macmillan Publishers Limited
London and Basingstoke
Associated companies throughout the world

ISBN 0-333-52099-8

Printed in Hong Kong

The Hardy family live next door, and Frankie Hardy is my best friend. We do everything together and last Christmas we were both shepherds in the school nativity play.

Mum and Dad came to watch, and so did Mr and Mrs
Hardy and Frankie's sister Susan. Mum said I spoke my
words very well, but Dad said that the tea towel wrapped
round my head looked just like a tea towel wrapped round
my head.

Mum told Dad to be quiet.

On the way home, the Hardys said that they didn't
know much about Christmas because they didn't have it
where they came from. Instead they had a Cheese Regatta
in the spring when everybody sailed in boats made out of
cheese. It was the Mouse New Year.

Dad said that sounded a lot less expensive than
Christmas – and Mum told him to be quiet again.

That night Dad explained to Frankie and Susan what Christmas was all about. He said it was a happy time of the year when families, friends and Father Christmas gave presents to celebrate the birth of Jesus – just like the Three Wise Men had done in the nativity play.

Frankie and Susan said they would like to have a Christmas, and Mr and Mrs Hardy said they would like to try one, too.

On the first day of the school holidays, Frankie and I
made Christmas decorations out of coloured paper. Susan
and Biscuit, our cat, tried to make some as well.

Dad seemed a bit fed up when he got back from work,

but Mum said our house was a home not an office, and that the decorations were lovely.

"The children made them all themselves," she said.

Mr Hardy came round after tea to ask if we had space for any more paper chains, because Frankie was still making them.

Two days later Dad struggled through the front door with an enormous Christmas tree. Mum said it was ridiculous, but Dad just grinned and said the house was a home not an office.

In the end he had to cut off the top of the tree so it could stand in our living room. He gave the top to the Hardys, and then said that that was what he had intended to do all along. I didn't believe him, and neither did Mum. That night Biscuit stole a chocolate snowman and was sick in the garden.

On the twenty-second of December we all went carol singing.
"You'll enjoy this," Dad told Mr Hardy. "It's very
traditional."

But we weren't out for very long. Susan whined all the
time because she was cold, I fell over a wall, and Biscuit,
who had come along for the fun, had a fight with another cat.

Dad didn't say anything when we got home.

Next day, Nan and Grandad arrived for Christmas.

The first thing Grandad said to me was that Christmas had been cancelled, but I knew he was joking because he says the same thing every year.

Nan immediately went into the kitchen and, even though Mum said she didn't need any help, Nan insisted. Nan is Dad's mum.

Nan hadn't been in the kitchen for more than five minutes when there was a terrible scream. We all ran in and found her standing on a chair pointing at Biscuit's catflap.

"A rat! A rat!" she shouted. "There was a rat at the door!"

"It wasn't a rat. It was a mouse," said Mum calmly. "Young Frankie often pops in to say hello."

"Pops in!" squealed Nan. "That dirty, whiskery thing! You surely don't let it walk around your house, do you?"

"Of course we do, Mother," said Dad. "Frankie and his family are friends and they're welcome any time."

"Well really," said Nan. "I've never heard anything like it. Whatever do the neighbours think?"

"They are our neighbours," said Dad.

A little later I went out and found Frankie and we
played in the garden. Just as I accidentally squashed
Frankie's football, Nan called me in for lunch.

"Make sure you scrub your nails thoroughly," she said
when I was washing my hands. "We don't want to catch
anything nasty now, do we?"

That night I heard Nan say that she had nothing against mice, pet ones or wild ones, but mice had their place and that place wasn't living next door. It shouldn't be allowed.

Dad was very quiet for a moment, and then he told Nan to remember it was Christmas time.

And suddenly it was Christmas! On the morning of
Christmas Eve I opened the last door on my advent
calendar and wrapped up the presents I had bought for
everyone.

In the evening, when it was dark, we all went to the
family carol service in St Mary's Church.

Nan was surprised to see so many mice families at the service, and she seemed to go all stiff when the Hardys came and sat next to us. All of a sudden she began to read her carol sheet very closely.

"Merry Christmas and how do you do?" said Mr Hardy to Nan and Grandad. "Frankie told us you'd arrived and we've been looking forward to meeting you."

"Good evening and Merry Christmas to you, too," said Grandad.

Nan just nodded, but all through the service she kept glancing at the Hardys while pretending to ignore them.

When we got home, she said, "Personally, I've got nothing against mice, but I do think they should keep to their own churches. It doesn't seem right that they should come and invade ours like that, even if they are well behaved."

I was very excited that night. Before I went to bed I left some sherry and a plate of carrots in the fireplace for Father Christmas and his reindeer, and I asked Dad not to put any more coal on the fire.

At one time I think I did hear the coal scuttle. But suddenly I felt something bumpy and crunchy on the end of my bed. I knew it was morning. Father Christmas had been.

In my stocking I got a puppet, a rubber that smelled of banana, a notebook, some coloured make-up sticks, a diary, a tangerine, some nuts, a torch, a gorilla mask, some false teeth, a chocolate snowman, a puzzle, another tangerine, a Batman pencil, and a pink sugar mouse.

Frankie and Susan got exactly the same in their stockings. They showed me.

Christmas morning always goes so slowly to start with.
I wanted to open the presents around the tree straight
away, but Mum said I couldn't go in the living room until she'd
hoovered and until Nan and Grandad had finished their breakfast.
   Nan eats toast very slowly – especially when she's knitting.
   "By the way, Mother," said Dad, as he finished his
coffee, "I just thought I'd tell you that the Hardys will be

dropping in this morning for an hour or so."

Nan sniffed. "I thought perhaps they would be," she said. "Well, I don't entirely approve, as you know, but neighbours are neighbours and I'd be polite to yours even if they were covered in green spots. It doesn't mean I have to like them, though. What time are they coming?"

"They are here now," I said, and I ran and opened the door.

At last the time had come. Dad told us to sit down in the living room, and then he gave out the presents from under the tree.

Everybody got exactly what they wanted. Even Biscuit got a squeaky fish which Mum had done up in ribbon.

Nan liked all her soap and things, but she seemed more interested in folding up all the wrapping paper and saving it for next year.

Grandad immediately smoked one of his cigars, and Biscuit got so excited with his fish that he had to go out in the garden.

When most of the boxes and rubbish had been pushed
to one side, Frankie walked over to Nan and tapped her
nervously on the shoe. He called her Nan.

He said, "Nan, this is for you. It's from all of us, but it was
me who wrapped it," and he quickly handed her a parcel.

"How very kind," said Nan, "and isn't it beautifully
wrapped? May I try to guess what's inside?"

Nan thanked the Hardys very much indeed for her
thimble. And Grandad was delighted with his pipe, too.
    Nan then reached into her basket.
    "And these are for you," she said. "They're not much,
but I do hope you like them."
    Mr and Mrs Hardy got a bedspread, Susan got a
cardigan and Frankie got a football. Nan had knitted them all.

A bit later, while Dad and Mr Hardy tried to get my robot to work, Mum, Nan and Mrs Hardy chatted together about all sorts of things. The New Year came up in the conversation, and so did the Mouse New Year and Cheese Regatta.

"You mean you actually sail in boats made out of Cheddar cheese?" said Nan. "Well, I had no idea. It just goes to show, you learn something new every day, don't you?"

"Why don't you come with us next time?" said Frankie. "There's always hundreds of mice there, and you'd enjoy it ever so much."

"Thank you, dear, I'm sure I would," said Nan hurriedly. "But don't you think I'd be a little big for the rest of you? I wouldn't really fit in, would I?"

"Well, you certainly wouldn't fit in a cheese boat," said Dad.

"No," said Grandad. "But I'd love to see her try."

And that made everybody laugh, including Nan.